World of Reading

MARVEL AVENGERS

This Is DOCTOR STRANGE and SCARLET WITCH

Adapted by **Emeli Juhlin**

Illustrated by **Steve Kurth**, **Geanes Holland**, *and* **Olga Lepaeva**

Based on the Marvel comic book characters **Doctor Strange** *and* **Scarlet Witch**

Los Angeles
New York

For information address Marvel Press, 77 West 66th Street, New York, New York, 10023.

Printed in the United States of America
First Edition, February 2022 10 9 8 7 6 5 4 3 2 1
Library of Congress Control Number: 2021931836
FAC-029261-21358
ISBN: 978-1-368-07020-1

This is Doctor Strange.
This is Scarlet Witch.

They can do magic.

Scarlet Witch lights
things on fire.

Doctor Strange puts out fires.

They live in New York City.

Everyone is under a spell!

Thunder booms.
The sky opens.

Dormammu is here.

He put a memory spell
on the heroes.

Doctor Strange
thinks about the past. . . .

He was a surgeon.

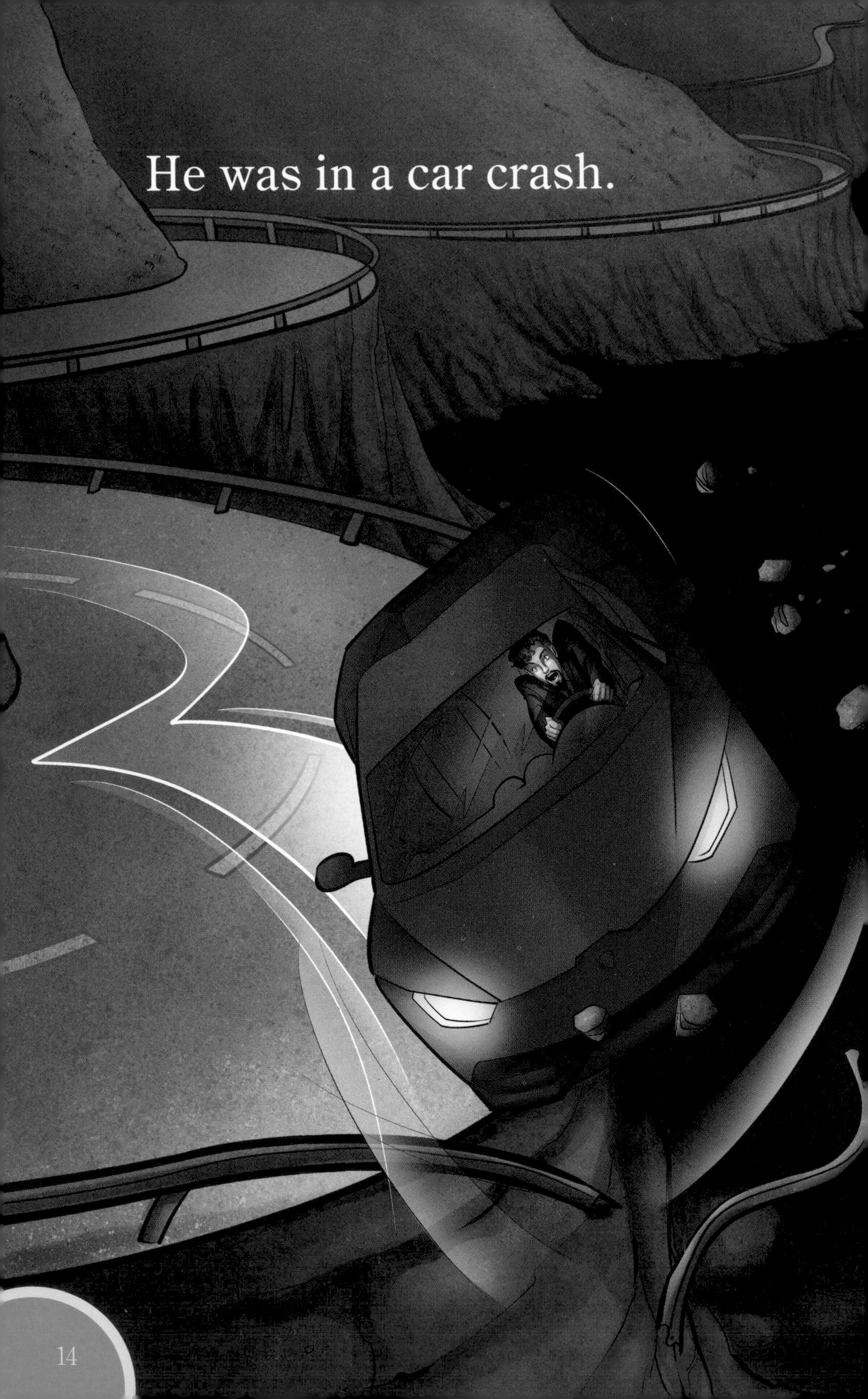

He was in a car crash.

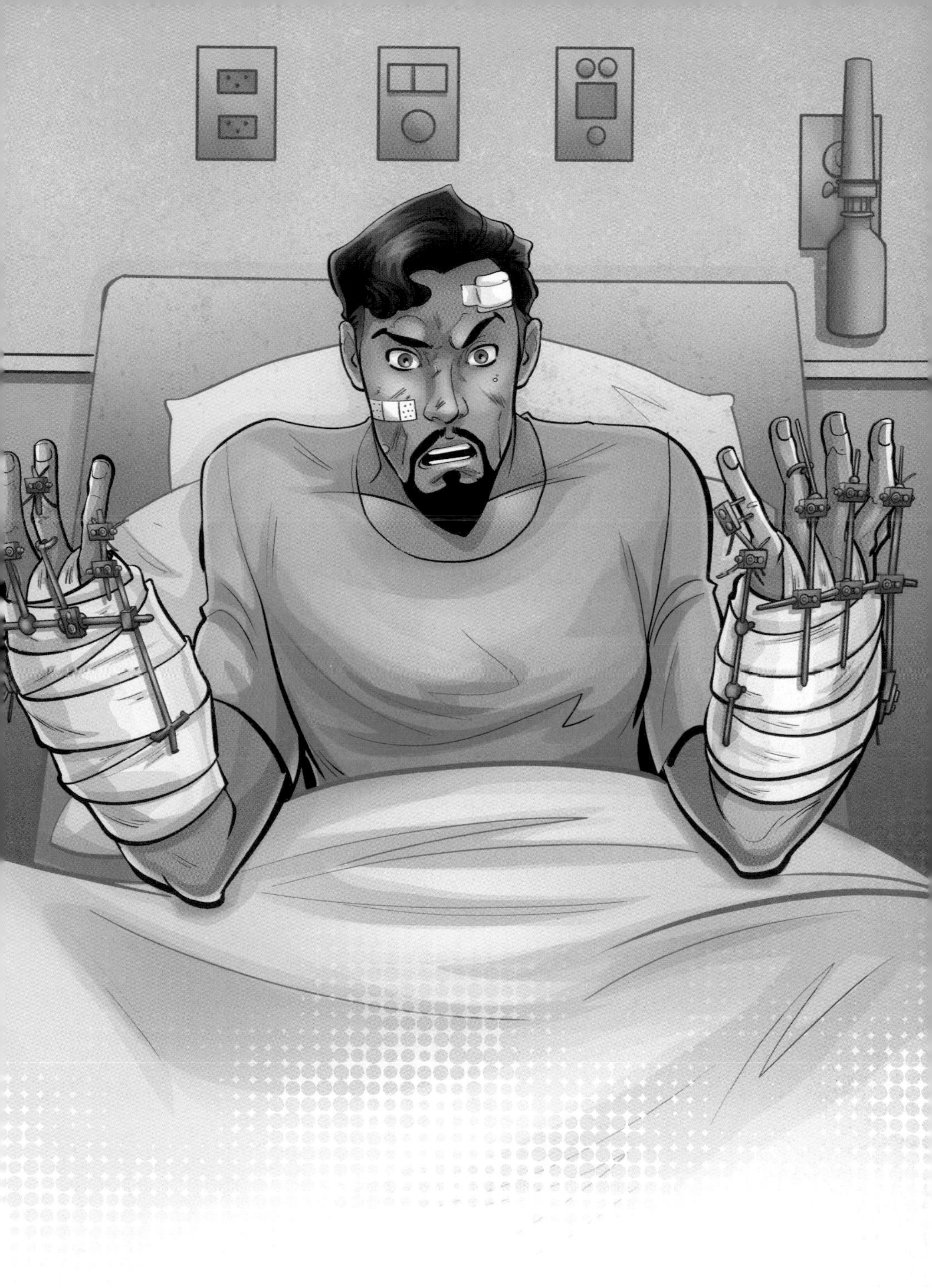

He hurt his hands.

He found magic.
He tried to fix his hands.

Doctor Strange uses
his magic for good.

But right now he can
only think about the past!

Scarlet Witch thinks
about the past. . . .
She was Wanda.
Pietro was her twin brother.

Wanda could do magic.
Pietro was very fast.

They looked out for each other.

Wanda became Scarlet Witch.
Pietro became Quicksilver.
They were villains.

Scarlet Witch met the Avengers.
She started using her magic
for good.
But right now she can only
think about the past!

The heroes know
they are under a spell.

Doctor Strange uses
his magic for good.
He is an Avenger!

Scarlet Witch uses her
magic for good.
She is an Avenger!

Doctor Strange and Scarlet Witch break the spell.

They work together.

Doctor Strange opens the sky.

Scarlet Witch sends the villain away.

Doctor Strange
and Scarlet Witch
save the day!